MR. MICK

written and illustrated by

STEVE AUGARDE

 ANDRE DEUTSCH

First published 1980 by
André Deutsch Limited
105 Great Russell Street London WC1

Copyright © 1980 by Steve Augarde
All rights reserved

Printed in Great Britain by
Sackville Press Billericay Ltd

British Library Cataloguing in Publication Data
Augarde, Steve
Mr Mick.
823'.9'1J   PZ7.A9125

ISBN 0-233-97254-4

Library of Congress Number 80-65660

Every Sunday was just the same.
After lunch Mr. Mick would put his feet up and snooze away the afternoon until tea-time. Mrs. Mick would put *her* feet up and snooze away the afternoon until tea-time. And the cat would put *its* feet up and snooze away the afternoon until tea-time.
It was one of those great days for snoozing, in fact.

And this particular Sunday afternoon started out pretty much as usual.
In went the lunch, up went the feet, and down went the eyelids. But could Mr. Mick sleep? No, he could not.
He shifted this way. He shifted that. No good.

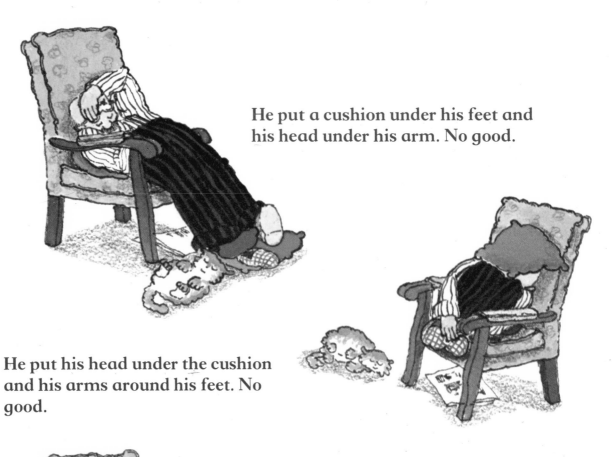

He put a cushion under his feet and his head under his arm. No good.

He put his head under the cushion and his arms around his feet. No good.

He put his head under a newspaper with his arm around a cushion and his feet under the cat. Still no good.

"It's no good," he said. "I can't sleep. Perhaps I should go for a walk instead."

"Good idea," said Mrs. Mick. "Good idea," thought the cat.

Mr. Mick rummaged around in the cupboard under the stairs.
"Where're my boots?" he said. "Who's had my cap? Anyone seen my stick?" He finally got himself organised and stumped off, leaving the house in peace and quiet.

There wasn't much going on in the town. All the shops were closed for Sunday and there was hardly anyone around. The holiday season hadn't begun yet.
Mr. Mick walked right through the old part of town and then past the new council estates to the outskirts.

It wasn't all that long before he was strolling out towards the countryside, swinging his stick and trying out his whistling, (which he didn't seem to have done for a long time).

Eventually he came to a small lane turning off from the main road. Pointing down the lane was a wooden sign that was so old and worn Mr. Mick could only just read it. TO THE TIP it said.

"'To the tip?'" thought Mr. Mick. "Tip of what? Reckon I'll take a look."

The lane was nothing more than an overgrown cinder track and as Mr. Mick walked along it he couldn't help noticing a bit of an unpleasant smell in the air.

Finally the track veered round to the right and, turning the corner, Mr. Mick was confronted with the biggest load of rubbish he'd ever seen. "Of course," he muttered. "A tip is a place where you dump rubbish. This is an old rubbish dump." And what a sight.

Busted sofas, broken bottles, tellys, stoves, oil drums, newspapers, toys, tin cans, an old piano, bicycles and bedsteads. You name it.
"Just about everything but the kitchen sink," thought Mr. Mick. Then he noticed a couple of those as well.

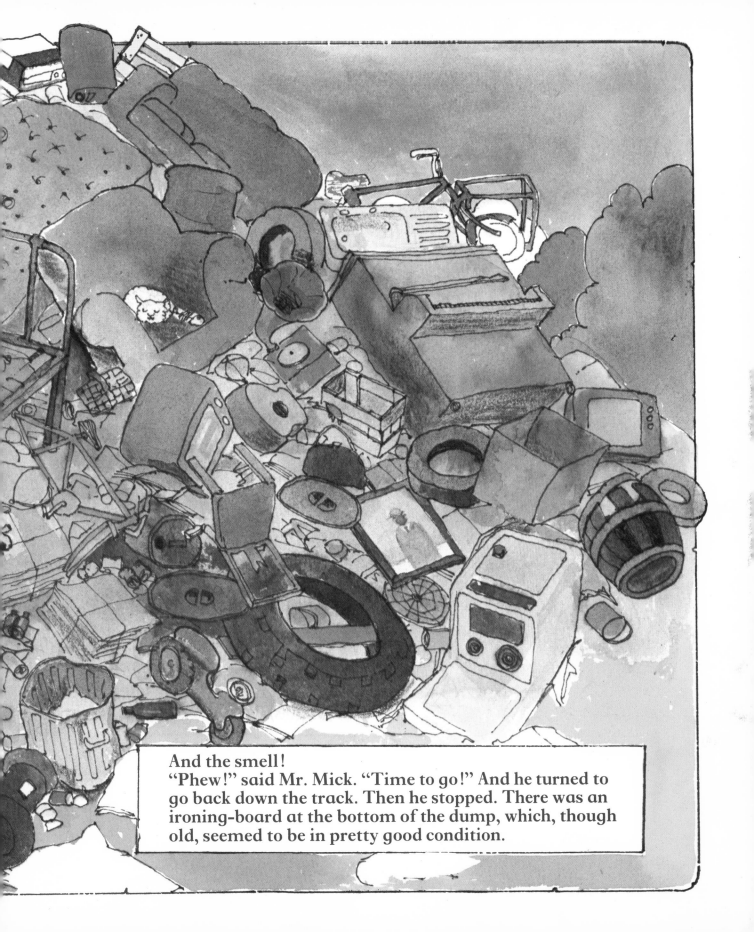

And the smell!
"Phew!" said Mr. Mick. "Time to go!" And he turned to
go back down the track. Then he stopped. There was an
ironing-board at the bottom of the dump, which, though
old, seemed to be in pretty good condition.

"Well, that's a bit of a waste," thought Mr. Mick. "I wonder if anyone could use that?"
He walked up to the ironing-board and gave it a bit of a prod with his stick.
"Hoi!" shouted a voice, "What's your game?"

Mr. Mick jumped about two feet into the air.
"Who's that?" he cried. "Who's there?"

"Me," said the ironing-board. "Just watch where you're
shoving that stick, that's all! Bloomin' cheek. And on a
Sunday, too! Can't a chap have a bit of peace?"
Then all the rest of the things on the rubbish dump started to
chime in as well.
"Yes, that's right! Leave us alone can't you? Shove off!"
Mr. Mick was amazed.
"I am amazed!" he said. "Bits of rubbish don't talk!"

"Who are you calling rubbish?" cried an old radio. "I'm in perfect working order, I am. I was forced into an early retirement, that's all. Nothing wrong with me!"

"Nor me!" shouted a grimy old copper kettle. "Couple of dents, perhaps. Nothing to worry about."

"What about me?" A funny-looking cuckoo clock piped up. "All I need is a bit of a clean up . . . good as new, I'd be!"

And gradually from all over the dump came voices claiming that, with a little care here and a bit of spit-and-polish there, they could soon be back in business.

"Hang on a minute," said Mr. Mick. "If there's really not much the matter with you then why have you been thrown away?"

"Oh, various reasons," said the ironing-board, moodily. "Mostly because we're old-fashioned I suppose. Not me, though. I was thrown away because of my short legs."

Mr. Mick noticed the ironing-board's short legs for the first time.

"I see," he said. "Er . . . were they always like that?"

"No, mate, they bloomin' well weren't!" said the ironing-board, hotly.

"Then tell us what happened," said Mr. Mick.

The Short-legged Ironing-board

"Well," said the ironing-board, "it was like this . . .
I was bought by a woman called Mrs. Little for her
husband to do the ironing on. Mr. Little didn't *like*
doing the ironing, but you could say that he didn't
have much choice in the matter. He did as he was
told.
The thing was, Mr. Little really *was* little. He was
so little, in fact, that when he was doing the
ironing, his chin hardly reached up to my height
and so he really couldn't see what he was doing.

Mrs. Little decided to help him, just to show that her heart was in the right place. She looked in her tool-box and got out a saw. And then, without any warning, she tipped me upside down and sawed my legs off until I was low enough for Mr. Little to do the ironing properly!

That wasn't the only help she gave him, mind. She also gave him a biscuit tin to stand on when he was doing the washing-up, so that he could see over the sink. And he had his own little set of brushes for when he had to sweep the chimney. She even made him a pair of stilts to wear when he pegged out the washing.

I think it was probably the stilts which gave Mr. Little the idea of running away to join the circus. Anyway, there he was one morning – gone, so to speak. Mrs. Little was furious. "After all the help I've given him!" she said.

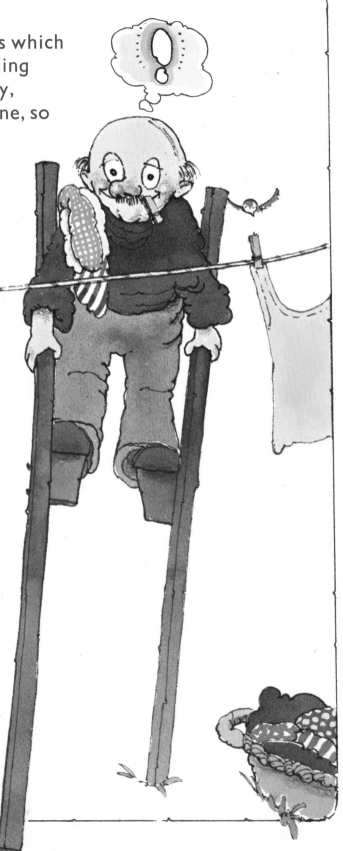

And so that was the end of it. It was also the end of it for me because I was so low down, what with my sawed-off legs, that when Mrs. Little tried to do the ironing it gave her a ricked back. So she threw me away."

"I see," said Mr. Mick. He looked at the old radio. "And what about you?" he said. "How did you get here?"

The Wooden Radio

"Well," said the radio, "it was like this. . . .
I was delivered, brand new from the shop, to a
farmer who lived by himself out in the country.
He never left his farm, you see, or had any visitors,
and all his family had grown up and gone abroad
so I was to be company for him.
He looked very pleased when I arrived. He dusted
off a shelf for me straight away, switched me on
and sat back in his chair to listen. It was six o'clock.
"Here is the six o'clock news," I said.
"Oh good," he said. "I haven't heard a bit of news
for years. It'll cheer me up. Go on."

"Taxes are expected to go up again soon," I said.
"Oh really?" he said. "That's a blow."
"Prices are rising," I said.
"Oh no!" he said.
"Especially prices of agricultural equipment."
"What? How dreadful!"
"A new form of potato-blight has broken out . . ."
"I can't believe it!"
". . . and is expected to spread all over the country."
"This is horrendous!"

"Weather experts say that the rain will continue for a month or so," I said.
"Heaven help us!" he moaned.
"Then there will probably be a drought."
"Mercy!"

"The bottom has fallen out of the pig market."
"A disaster!"
"And nobody wants any more milk."
"What?" cried the farmer. "This is the last straw! I had no idea that the country was in such a state! I'm leaving!"
And he emigrated. He sold his farm and joined his family abroad, stopping just long enough on the way to throw me on the rubbish dump. And that was that."

"I see," said Mr. Mick. "And what about you?" he said to the copper kettle. "What's your story?"

The Whistling Copper kettle

"Well," said the kettle, "it was like this. . . . .
I'd just started work in a big posh house. My first night, it was, and everyone had gone to bed. I was down in the kitchen in the dark. Suddenly there was this torch flashing about the place. A burglar! Well, he bumped around the kitchen for a few minutes, looking at this and that, and then what do you think he finally stole? Me! A kettle!

He put me in his sack and off we went.
The next thing I knew, we were back at his place and he was pulling me out of the sack to show to his wife.
"Look at this, my lovely," he cried. "A kettle! Just what we needed, eh? What a haul!"
"Oh Bigsby," said his wife. "You're the worst burglar I ever saw! Why can't you be like other burglars? What good is a kettle? You should be burgling jewels or paintings, not kettles."
"Jewels?" said Bigsby-the-Burglar. "Jewels? You can't make a nice cup of tea out of jewels! *Or* paintings. Can't boil up your shaving-water in a painting, now can you? No. But a kettle, now that's really useful.

And look at this, it's real copper! *And* it's got a whistle!''
He was really proud of me, you could tell.
''Well, well,'' he said. ''I think I shall just brew myself a nice cup of tea. Using my new whistling copper kettle. Heh heh.''
''Well, I'm going back to bed,'' said his wife. ''You daft old burglar, you.''

Bigsby-the-Burglar filled me up with water and put me on the stove to boil. Then he sat down by the stove. Then he fell asleep. By the time I was ready to boil he was snoring away quite loudly. So I gave him the biggest whistle I could, to wake him up. "PEEEEEEEEEEEPPP!!"I went.
"AAAARRRRGGGGHHHH!!" he yelled, leaping up. "POLICE!!"
And he dived out of the window.

"Perhaps you're right, my lovely, perhaps you're right," said Bigsby-the-Burglar to his wife the next morning. "Maybe I should give up burgling altogether. My nerves aren't what they used to be. And I'm afraid that whistling copper kettle will have to go. I think I'll throw it on the dump later on."

"Oh? Why's that?" said his wife.

"Because, my lovely," said Bigsby-the-Burglar, "That whistling copper kettle sounds just like a copper, whistling."

"And that's how I came to be here," said the kettle.
"I see," said Mr. Mick. "Well, well, well."

And so, one by one, the bits and pieces on the rubbish dump told their stories to Mr. Mick. Mostly, it seemed, they had been thrown away because they were old-fashioned.

"How can we compete?" they said.

It was true that some of the things were very old and out-dated compared with modern goods. There was a wind-up record-player, with a big tin horn where the sound came out.

There was a washboard and an old mangle which had been used to wring out clothes before the days of the washing-machine and the spin-drier. There was a big box-camera on a wooden tripod, a child's rocking horse, a butcher-boy's bicycle, an enamel jug and wash-basin – lots of funny looking things. None of it was like the stuff you see nowadays. But this was what gave Mr. Mick his idea.

"Listen," he said, "I've had a bit of a brainwave! Come home with me and meet the wife and I'll show you what we'll do." And so it was settled. Mr. Mick borrowed an old van from a mate and went to and fro, carrying bits of junk from the disused dump back to his place. When he told Mrs. Mick about his plan she was all for it and so together they got down to work.

They hammered, scraped, polished, rubbed and scrubbed. They dusted, brushed, washed, wiped and dried. They nailed, sawed, drilled, stitched and sewed. Finally, they painted.
They painted a big sign which read . . .

And they put the sign over their front door. They had opened an antique shop!

All the bits and pieces from the rubbish dump were there in the window or standing outside. Polished and mended. Just like new. Or rather – just like old. "Real Antiques".

And of course the shop was a great success. It still puzzles Mr. Mick a bit, though.

"After all," he says, "if people are so keen to buy back the stuff they once threw away – then why throw it away in the first place?"

Good question.